ISBN 0 86112 872 9
© Brimax Books Ltd 1988.
All rights reserved.
Brimax Paperbacks edition first published 1992.
Second printing 1992.
Brimax Paperbacks is an imprint of Brimax Books Ltd,
Newmarket, England.
Printed in Portugal.

The Forgetful Spider

by June Woodman
Illustrated by Ken Morton

BRIMAX PAPERBACKS

Spider is putting on his shoes.
He is going to Kangaroo's
party. He counts his shoes
as he puts them on.
"One, two, three, four, five,
six, seven . . ." Only seven
shoes for EIGHT feet!
"Oh dear, I have lost one
of my shoes," says Spider.
He looks in his house but he
cannot find the shoe anywhere.

He goes to look for the shoe.
He meets Elephant. Elephant
is busy picking oranges.
"Hello, Elephant. Have you seen
my shoe?" asks Spider.
"No," says Elephant, "and I am
far too busy to look for it.
If you see Alligator, tell
him I will bring oranges
to Kangaroo's party."
"I shall probably forget,"
says Spider.

Spider sets off to look for
Alligator. As he runs along,
one shiny shoe falls off.
Spider does not see it.
Alligator is on the muddy
river bank.
"Hello, Spider," shouts
Alligator. He waves his tail.
SPLOSH! The mud splashes
spider's shiny shoes.

Spider forgets all about
the oranges.
"Look at my shoes!" he cries.
"They are not shiny now."
"Sorry, Spider," says Alligator.
Spider counts his shoes.
"One, two, three, four,
five, six . . ."
"You have lost two shoes,"
says Alligator.
"Have you seen them?"
asks Spider.
"No," says Alligator.

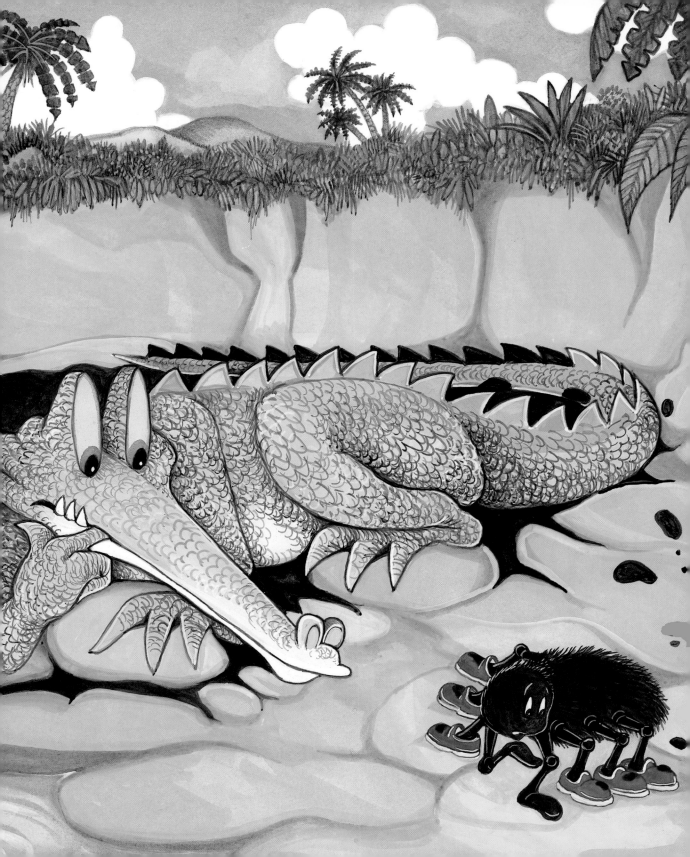

"Go and ask Mouse," says
Alligator, "and tell her
I will bring a cake
to Kangaroo's party."
"I shall probably forget,"
says Spider. He sets off
to look for Mouse. As he
runs along, another shoe
falls off. But Spider
does not see it.

Boom! Boom! Boom!
It is Mouse. She is playing
her drum. What a noise!
"Hey Spider!" says Mouse.
"Where are your shoes?"
Spider forgets all about the
cake. He counts his shoes again.
"One, two, three, four, five."
Only five shoes for eight feet.

"I have lost three shoes now,"
says Spider. "Do you know
where they are?"
"No," says Mouse. "Have you
asked Lion? Maybe he can
help. If you see Lion, tell him
I will take my drum
to Kangaroo's party."
"I shall probably forget,"
says Spider.

Spider sets off again.
As he runs, another shoe
falls off. He does not see it.
There is Lion. He is asleep,
as usual, under a tree.
Lion opens one eye.
"Hello, Spider. You have lost
four of your shoes," he says.

Spider forgets about the drum.
"Oh, not another shoe," cries
Spider. He counts his shoes.
"One, two, three, four . . ."
Four shoes for EIGHT feet.
Lion is much too tired
to help Spider look for them.
"Ask Kangaroo," says Lion
with a yawn. "She may know."

"Oh, Spider," says Lion, "tell Kangaroo I will bring flowers to her party."
"I shall probably forget," says Spider. As he runs off, another shoe falls off.
But still he does not see! He meets Kangaroo.
"Hello, Spider. Where are your shoes?" she cries.

Spider forgets about the flowers.
He counts his shoes.
''One, two, three . . .''
Only three shoes left.
Spider begins to cry
''Cheer up, Spider,'' says
Kangaroo. ''You are just in time
for my party.''
''Party?'' sobs Spider. ''Oh dear,
I forgot about your party.''

Look. Here comes Elephant.
He is carrying some oranges
and one of Spider's shoes.
Along comes Alligator with
a cake and another shoe.
There is Mouse carrying her drum
and another shoe. Lion has
some flowers and another shoe.
Spider begins to count.
"I have three shoes. That makes
four . . . five . . . six . . . seven."

Poor Spider. Still only
seven shoes for eight feet.
But Kangaroo says, "Hey Spider.
Look in my pouch."
There is the lost shoe.
"Remember! You gave it to me
yesterday to clean it,"
says Kangaroo. "Bring me
the other seven tomorrow
and I will clean them too."
"Thank you," says Spider,
"but I shall probably forget."

Here are some words in the story.

counts	muddy
lost	another
busy	asleep
party	opens
forget	tired
shiny	yawn
falls	pouch

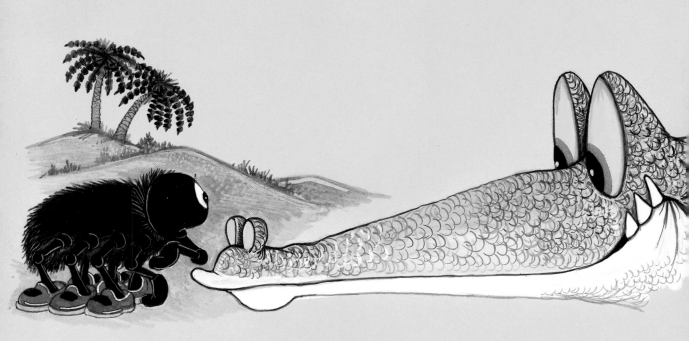

Here are some pictures in the story.

shoes

oranges

cake

drum

flowers